Blue's Clues™

Blue's Egg Hunt

by Deborah Reber
illustrated by Carolyn Norden

SCHOLASTIC INC.
New York Toronto London Auckland Sydney
Mexico City New Delhi Hong Kong

To David and Barbara Basden ... my wonderful new family!—D. R.

For Charlotte.—C.N.

Note to Parents

It's springtime at Blue's Clues, and Steve and Blue are bringing their new neighbor Periwinkl along with them to the spring fair. In this book your child can help the Blue's Clues crew mak their leaf prints, pick out their spring hats, and find hidden eggs at the fair to win a big prize!

Based on the TV series *Blue's Clues*® created by Traci Paige Johnson, Todd Kessler,
and Angela C. Santomero as seen on Nick Jr.®
On *Blue's Clues*, Steve is played by Steven Burns.

ISBN 0-439-28036-2

Published by Scholastic Inc., 555 Broadway, New York, NY 10012, by arrangement with Simon Spotlight, an imprint of Simon & Schuster Children's Publishing Division.

12 11 10 9 8 7 6 5 4 3 2 1 1 2 3 4 5 6/0

Printed in the U.S.A.

First Scholastic printing, April 2001

Hi there! You're here just in time. Blue and I were just about to head off to the spring fair on this lovely day. Would you like to come with us? Great! Let's go.

Periwinkle! What are you doing here?

Nothing to do? But it's a beautiful spring day.

What's so great about spring?

What's so great about spring? Well, there are flowers and blue sky and birds and . . . and . . . hey, I have an idea! Why don't you come with us to the spring fair?

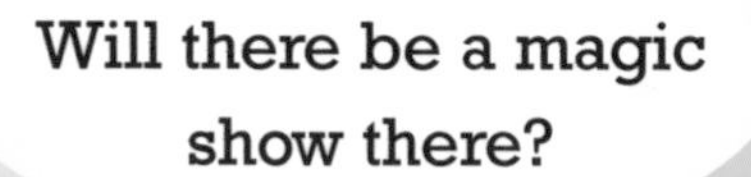

I don't know about that, but I'm sure there will be lots of other cool things to do. Come on! Let's go!

SPRING FAIR

We're here! Oh, I almost forgot. Keep a look out for hidden eggs. We're going to try to win the egg hunt this year, and we could really use your help.

leaf printing

Cool! Looking for hidden things is almost like magic. And I *love* magic.

So, what should we do first? I know, let's go to the first booth we see. So, which one is that? Yeah! The leaf printing booth.

Cool! I love making leaf prints! And it looks like they have all of our favorite colors of paint to use too. Green, blue, and . . .

. . . periwinkle! And I want to use a big round leaf for my print.

Good idea, Periwinkle.
And Blue and I like using long
thin leaves. Can you help us find the
perfect leaves to make our leaf prints?

Those are some great leaves you picked out! How do our leaf prints look? Let's take them home and put them up on the refrigerator.

Oh, I almost forgot. Did you find any eggs yet? You did? Great! Let's see if we can find some more! Hey . . . what's over there? A spring hat stand! My favorite. Let's go!

Wow! Look at all of these homemade hats. Since this is your *first* spring fair, Periwinkle, you should choose first. What animal do you want to be?

Well, I've always wanted to fly. How about an animal that can fly?

Sounds good to me. And I think I'll be a rabbit. What does Blue want to be? Oh! Blue wants to be a duck. So, we need a rabbit hat, a duck hat, and a hat for an animal that flies. Can you find hats for us?

So, this is what it feels like to be a rabbit!

I think Periwinkle is starting to like springtime. What about you? By the way, did you find any more eggs? Whoever finds the most hidden eggs gets a prize at the end of the fair. So, let's keep looking.

I want to grow some tomatoes.
tomato
tomato
peppers
peppers
cucumbers
cucumbers

And I'll plant some carrots. 'Cause, you know, rabbits *love* carrots. How about you, Blue? Lettuce? Sounds good to me. Can you help us find the seeds that we need to plant our garden?

Hey, Periwinkle! Blue! Come on over! We're about to announce the winner of the egg hunt contest. It looks like Purple Kangaroo and Green Puppy have the most eggs so far—eleven eggs.

So, if we have more than eleven eggs, we'll win the contest!

Do we have enough eggs to win?

We did it! Great job! Thanks for your help finding all those eggs. And look what we won—a garden kit! Periwinkle, let's plant a garden in your backyard, so you can enjoy a little bit of spring every day.

My own garden?
All right!